Dedications:

The Kalapana Cats
—*Carolyn Everett Han*

For Tomless
—*C. H. M.*

Half of the proceeds that I receive from the sale of
KALAPANA will be donated to the Humane Society.
—*Carolyn Everett Han*

Published and distributed by

ISLAND HERITAGE
P U B L I S H I N G

99-880 IWAENA STREET, AIEA, HAWAII 96701-3202
PHONE: (808) 487-7299 • FAX: (808) 488-2279
EMAIL: hawaii4u@islandheritage.com

ISBN#: 0-89610-326-9
First Edition, Second Printing - 2000

KALAPANA

Written by Carolyn Everett Han
Illustrated by Carole Hinds McCarty

ISLAND HERITAGE

2

Hawai'i is home to Pele, Goddess of Fire. Pele gives and she takes away. One night without warning, Pele ignited Kilauea Volcano. Shimmering fountains of red-hot lava danced in the sky. Eruptions shook the island. Billowing steam clouds hissed as rivers of melted rock poured down the mountain and into the sea.

Day after day, raging rivers of molten lava flowed down the mountainside. Thick, black ribbons crisscrossed the land. The unstoppable lava forced families to pack their belongings and leave their homes. Some had to leave their pets.

The fast, fiery fingers of lava chased a frightened kitten who had been left behind. Although the kitten stayed ahead of the flows, he was badly burned. His feet were burned. His ears and nose were burned. It was impossible to tell the color of his fur.

People along the road watched helplessly as crackling rocks hurled through the air. At last the kitten reached safety, exhausted and nearly dead. Even though no one thought he would live, a woman took him home. She put 'aloe on his burns. She gave him food and water. He was named Kalapana, after the place where she found him.

Kalapana healed. Fluffy white fur with gray heart-shaped patches soon covered his body. His nose looked like pink velvet and his golden eyes twinkled again. Kalapana appreciated all the help the woman gave him, but he did not stay.

For days Kalapana walked. If the sun got too hot, he rested in the shade of *kukui* trees. When it rained, he found shelter under *'ape* leaves. At night, he slept curled up in the fragrant ginger patches. Kalapana did not know what he was searching for, but he would know when he found it.

One afternoon, Kalapana passed a papaya farm and saw a girl with long dark braids. When she leaned over a basket of golden fruit, he rubbed against her legs. Surprised by the kitten, she asked, "Are you lost?" Then she picked him up. While Kalapana dangled in midair, they looked into each other's eyes. "May I keep him?" Pua begged her mother. Kalapana stayed.

15

Life as a farm cat was good. Kalapana played in the papaya fields, enjoying the rain and sunshine. He chased birds and mice — mostly as a game — but sometimes he caught them. At night, Kalapana curled up on Pua's bed and Pua read him stories until they both fell sound asleep.

Over the years Pua and Kalapana grew and changed. The family moved to Hilo, the largest town on the Big Island. Being a Hilo cat was wonderful. When it rained Kalapana watched the world from a window. If it was sunny he took long naps on the covered *lānai*. After dinner Kalapana walked around the neighborhood saying "*Aloha*" to his many friends.

One evening before bedtime, Pua and Kalapana sat outside and watched the twinkling stars in the ever-changing Hawaiian night sky. Pua knew that Kalapana was getting old. Holding him close and petting his silky, but thinning, fur, Pua could not imagine life without Kalapana.

In May, just before the mangos ripened, Pua was sad—sadder than she had ever been. Kalapana was sick. Then one morning he did not wake up. Pua lined Kalapana's grave with *ti* leaves and placed him in the ground. For days Pua's tears fell and mixed with Pele's tears which rained from the sky. Together their tears watered the hibiscus bush that Pua had planted on Kalapana's grave.

After school Pua cared for the hibiscus. She waited and watched for a sign. Finally, a big orange flower appeared. Pua knew that Kalapana was happy because the inside of the flower's center was EXACTLY the color as his velvety pink nose.

In spring, Pua saw a green caterpillar nibbling the glossy leaves. Later she found a silver chrysalis dangling from a stem. Inside the chrysalis amazing changes were taking place. One sunny morning the silver sack split open and out popped a white butterfly with tiny gray hearts on its wings. Pua smiled as she watched "Kalapana" fly.

One stormy winter day, Pua glanced out the rain-streaked window to say "*Aloha*" to her "Kalapana bush." But it was gone! She raced out the door and down the steps. The hibiscus bush was lying on the ground, torn apart by the wind. Pua gathered up the broken pieces and carried them inside.

Hugging the torn branches in her arms, Pua sobbed. While her tears washed the crumpled leaves, she remembered Kalapana in his many forms: a kitten, a cat, a flower, and a butterfly. Then she had an idea—"I'll take cuttings from the branches!" Carefully she clipped twelve stems and planted them in pots. When Pua finished, she had a dozen little "Kalapana plants" sitting in a row.

Pua loved her small hibiscus plants. When they grew big enough, she gave them to friends. Her friends made cuttings, and the cycle continued. Today, hundreds of "Kalapana" hibiscus bushes with big velvety pink-centered orange flowers grow in Hawai'i.

Later Pua wrote Kalapana's story. In this way, he lives in words. What Pua learned from Pele and Kalapana is that nothing ever dies—it only changes form.

GLOSSARY

'Aloe   A thick, plump plant with clear gel inside the leaves. The gel has many medicinal uses.

Aloha   An affectionate Hawaiian greeting with many meanings — hello, goodbye, peace, love, or please return.

'Ape   The Hawaiian word for plants with big green leaves that look like elephant ears.

Ginger   An exotic, fragrant flower. Many varieties grow in Hawai'i — white, yellow, pink, and red.

Hibiscus   Hawai'i's state flower.

Kilauea   World's largest erupting volcano, located on the island of Hawai'i.

Kukui   A leafy tree with clusters of nuts, also called the candlenut tree. The nuts are used for candles, medicine, and jewelry.

Lānai   A balcony or deck attached to a house.

Mango   Yellowish red oblong-shaped fruit with thick rind, one flat seed, and juicy, orange-colored flesh. Mangos grow on big leafy trees.

Papaya   Large yellowish-green fruit that is eaten raw or cooked. Papayas grow in clusters on the top of tall, hollow trunks that are topped with broad green leaves.

Pele   Goddess of the Volcano. In Hawaiian mythology, she created the Hawaiian Islands.

Pua   Means "flower" in Hawaiian and is frequently used as a girl's name.

Ti   A plant with slender stalks and long, narrow green or red leaves. In Hawai'i, ti plants are said to bring good luck. The leaves have many uses.

Although the volcanic island of Hawai'i
is approximately 700,000 years old,
it is the youngest and biggest in the Hawaiian Archipelago
or chain that stretches for 1,523 miles.
Fondly known as the Big Island,
it is bigger than all of the other Hawaiian Islands combined.

Kaua'i

O'ahu

Moloka'i

Maui

Lāna'i

Major Hawaiian Islands

Hāwī

Kawaihae

Waimea

Hawai'i

Cartography by T. R. Paradise

Kailua-Kona

Hilo

Kapoho

Kealakekua

Kalapana

Hawai'i

Ka Lae